ARNOLD'S

EXTRAORDINARY ART

MUSEUM

CATHERINE INGRAM
& JIM STOTEN

LAURENCE KING PUBLISHING

ARNOLD'S EXTRAORDINARY ART MUSEUM
FEATURING:

ARNOLD

COLLECTOR AND CURATOR OF THE ART MUSEUM. TIDY, HIGHLY ORGANIZED, AND VERY BOSSY, ARNOLD NEVERTHELESS IMPRESSES WITH HIS BRIEFCASE OF ART TOOLS AND, OF COURSE, WITH HIS FABULOUS COLLECTION OF ART.

DOT

CURIOUS DOT HAS PLENTY OF QUESTIONS, BUT THE YOUNGEST MEMBER OF THE GANG REALLY PREFERS TO CHECK THINGS OUT FOR HERSELF. SHE IS EXTREMELY FOND OF HER BEDRAGGLED TEDDY, HER FAVORITE COLOR IS DEFINITELY RED, AND SHE HATES THE DARK.

GEORGE

AN A-STAR STUDENT AND CHAMPION FLUTE PLAYER, GEORGE IS ARNOLD'S BEST FRIEND AND HAPPY TO DROP EVERYTHING TO HELP HIM OPEN THE MUSEUM TO A NEW GROUP OF FRIENDS.

SPIKE

AN ACE SKATEBOARDER KNOWN FOR HIS GRAND SLIDES, SPIKE CAN USUALLY BE FOUND DOWN AT THE LOCAL SKATE PARK UNLESS HE IS REFUELING AT THE LOCAL CAFÉ, MUNCHING DOWN ONE OF HIS FAVORITE PEANUT BUTTER, JELLY, AND GHERKIN SANDWICHES.

GERTRUDE

GERTRUDE CAN BE A BIT OF A GRUMP. A KEEN ARTIST HERSELF, SHE LIKES DRAWING IN PURPLE BIRO AND IS SECRETLY IMPRESSED BY ARNOLD'S WORLD. SHE OCCASIONALLY BABYSITS FOR LITTLE DOT, AND ALTHOUGH SHE LIKES TO PLAY IT COOL, SHE ALWAYS LOOKS OUT FOR HER.

OCELOT

VERY MUCH A FREE SPIRIT, NO ONE IS QUITE SURE WHERE OCELOT CAME FROM. PERHAPS HE'S AN ESCAPEE FROM THE ZOO? THIS CAT LIKES TO DO THINGS IN HIS OWN WAY AND AT HIS OWN PACE.

BUG

LIKE OCELOT, LITTLE IS KNOWN ABOUT BUG AND WHERE HE CAME FROM. BUT EVERYONE AGREES THAT HE MUST ALWAYS BE THERE. HE IS THE MUSEUM'S SELF-APPOINTED PHOTOGRAPHER.

7

COME ON, GUYS, GIVE ARNOLD A CHANCE...

FOR A LONG TIME THERE WASN'T A PURE BLUE PAINT.

THAT'S SILLY, ARNOLD. HOW DID THEY PAINT BLUEBERRIES OR BLUEBELLS?

AND THEN PEOPLE HEARD OF THE PRECIOUS LAPIS LAZULI STONE...

FROM THE CAVES OF AFGHANISTAN.

IT'S TRUE, WE MINED THE STONE AND GROUND IT UP...

INTO A BLUE POWDER.

AND THEN...

MERCHANTS TRAVELED 3,750 MILES TO VENICE WHERE THEY SOLD THEIR PRECIOUS BLUE FOR GOLD.

THAT'S REALLY FAR.

BUT WHAT DID HE DO WITH THIS NEW BLUE?

WELL, HE DECIDED THAT HE WANTED TO SHARE IT AFTER ALL.

HE SENT SPECIAL INVITATIONS WITH SPECIAL BLUE STAMPS...

INVITING PEOPLE TO HIS EXHIBITIONS OF BLUE ART.

ONCE HE SERVED BLUE DRINKS TO ALL HIS GUESTS...

AND AFTERWARD THEIR PEE WAS BLUE.

AND HERE I HAVE RECREATED KLEIN'S FLOOR OF BLUE.

DOT'S OFF.

WHAT'S YOUR NAME?

RACHEL WHITEREAD. CALL ME RACHEL.

RACHEL, DO YOU PREFER PAINTING DINOSAURS OR PRINCESSES?

ERR... DOES ANYONE ELSE HAVE A QUESTION?

IT'S OK, ARNOLD. I CAN ONLY DRAW WHAT IS INSIDE MYSELF.

SOMETIMES I'M A DINOSAUR AND VERY OCCASIONALLY I'M A PRINCESS.

REALLY THOUGH, WHAT INTERESTS ME IS THE HIDDEN, FORGOTTEN SPACES WE LIVE IN. TAKE THIS MATCHBOX.

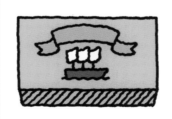

IMAGINE THE MATCHBOX CLOSED...

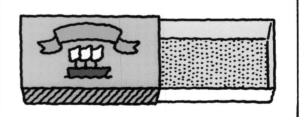

THEN IMAGINE IT OPEN. THAT INSIDE SPACE—THAT FASCINATES ME.

BUT I WORK ON A LARGE SCALE. LET ME SHOW YOU...

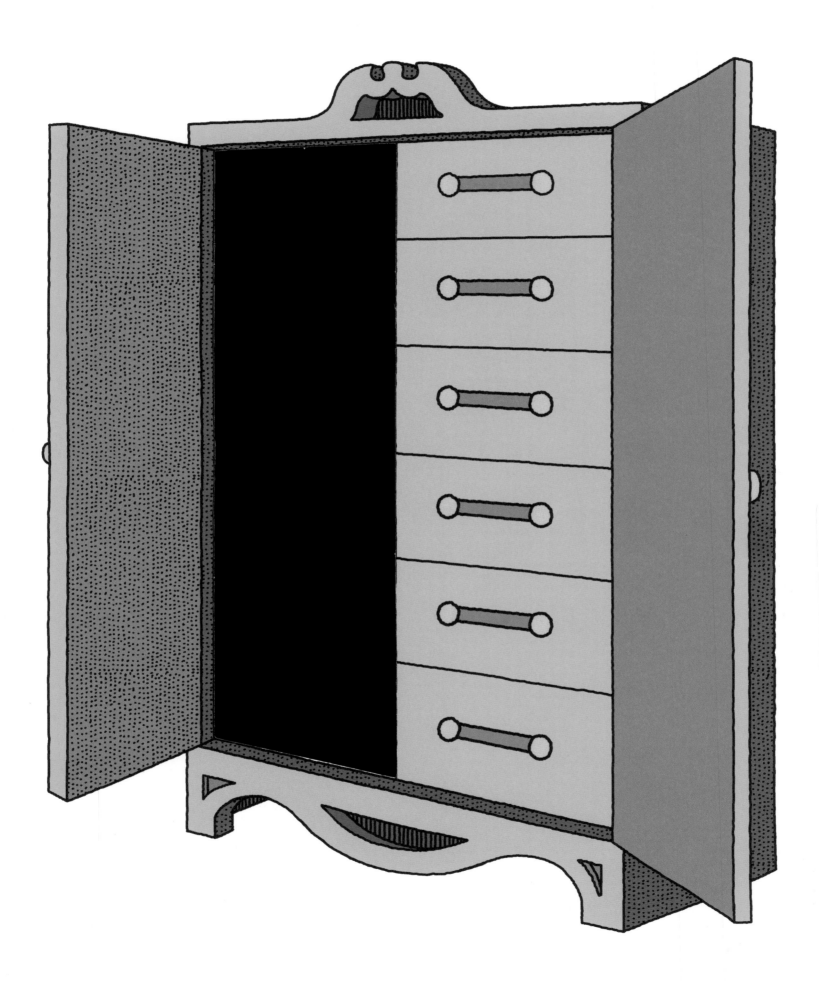

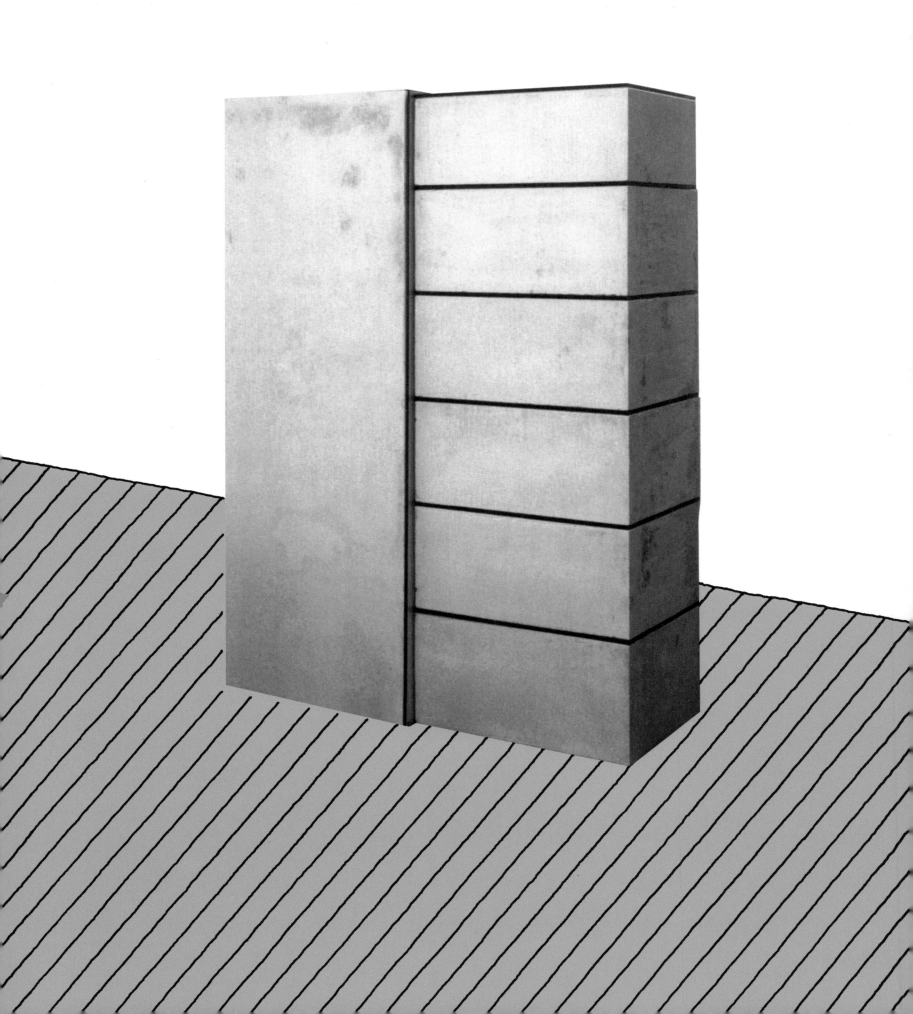

40

DOT?

I'M TIRED.

PABLO PICASSO MADE THE NEXT PIECE DURING WORLD WAR II. FOR OPTIMUM VIEWING, RECREATING PARIS IN A WARTIME BLACKOUT, THE NEXT ROOM WILL BE COMPLETELY DARK.

THE DARK?! AGAIN!?

OUCH
SORRY!
COME THIS WAY, GUYS.
REALLY, REALLY SCARED! LIKE WHEN I HAVE TO READ ALOUD OR EAT PEAS!

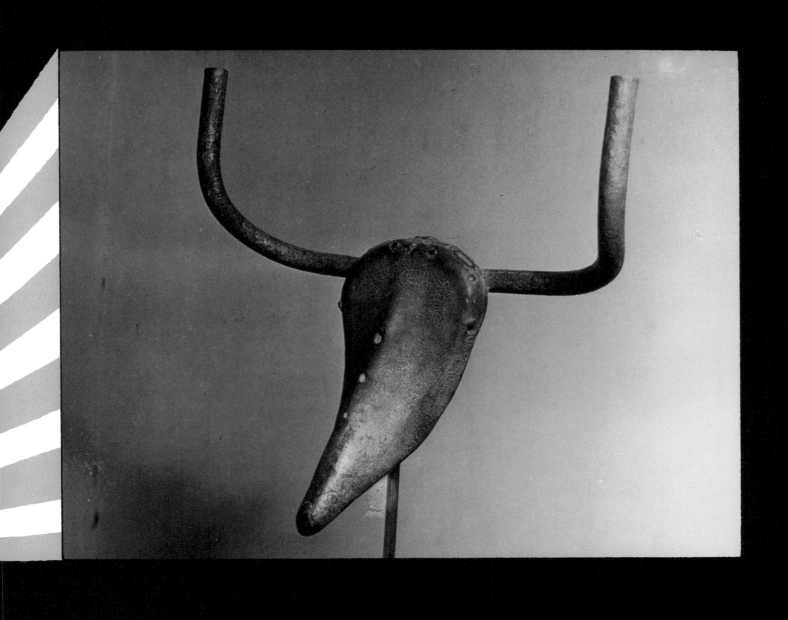

BACK IN THE LIGHT!

WE ARE COMING UP TO OUR LAST WORK...

A HAPPENING.

OOOOH! NOW I'M NOT TIRED!

SO THE LAST WORK IS...

IT'S A PARTY!

WILL THERE BE CAKE?

NO, BUT THERE WILL BE MUSIC...

AND THERE WILL BE DRESSING UP!

WE ARE GOING TO RE—LIVE THE BAUHAUS METAL PARTY, WHICH WAS HELD ON FEBRUARY 9TH, 1929, AT THE FAMOUS BAUHAUS ART SCHOOL IN GERMANY.

A METAL PARTY!?!?!?!?!

THE STUDENTS AND TEACHERS OF THE BAUHAUS THOUGHT OUT AND DESIGNED EVERY ELEMENT OF THEIR PARTY. LOOK, HERE'S THE INVITATION.

Piero Manzoni (1933–1963),
Merda d'artista, No 14, May 1961.

Metal, paper, and "artist's poop,"
1⅞ x 2½ in (4.8 x 6.5 cm).
Gift of Jo Carole and Ronald S. Lauder.
The Museum of Modern Art.
Digital image, The Museum of Modern Art,
New York/Scala Florence. © DACS 2016.

Marcel Duchamp (1887–1968),
Fountain, 1917 (replica 1964).

Porcelain,
12 x 15 x 18 in (30.5 x 38.1 x 45.7 cm).
Philadelphia Museum of Art. Gift (by exchange)
of Mrs. Herbert Cameron Morris, 1998.
Photo: The Philadelphia Museum of Art/Art Resource/Scala,
Florence. © Succession Marcel Duchamp/ADAGP, Paris and
DACS, London 2016.

Giovanni Bellini (c. 1430–1516),
The Madonna of the Meadow, c. 1500.

Oil and egg on synthetic panel, transferred from wood,
26½ x 34 in (67.3 x 86.4 cm).
Bought 1858. The National Gallery, London.
© The National Gallery, London/Scala, Florence.

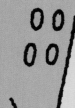

YOU'VE BEEN LOOKING AT:

Narcissus bulb bowl,
China, Song dynasty (960–1279).

Repaired with gold lacquer in Japan
Jun ware, glazed stoneware,
diameter 8 in (20 cm)
Ashmolean Museum, Oxford.

Jackson Pollock (1912–1956),
Autumn Rhythm (Number 30), 1950.

Enamel on canvas,
105 x 207 in (266.7 x 525.8 cm).
George A. Hearn Fund, 1957 (57.92).
Metropolitan Museum of Art, New York.
Image copyright The Metropolitan Museum of Art/Art
Resource/Scala, Florence.
© The Pollock/Krasner Foundation ARS, NY and DACS,
London 2016.

Yves Klein (1928–1962),
Blue Monochrome, 1961.

Dry pigment in synthetic polymer medium
on cotton over plywood,
76⅞ x 55⅛ in (195.1 x 140 cm).
The Sidney and Harriet Janis Collection. 618.1967.
The Museum of Modern Art, New York.
© Yves Klein, ADAGP, Paris and DACS, London 2016.

Natalia Goncharova (1881–1962),
Costume for the Prince in the ballet
Sadko, 1916.

Long tunic of scarlet velvet and satin, with high wired
orange silk collar, appliqued with gold tissue 'sunflowers'
and foliage, bands of simulated gold frogging, and a hem
band of chrome-yellow silk with scarlet and white
'crown' pattern. High-crowned cap with padded rim of
copper-coloured silk, crimson velvet and scarlet silk,
trimmed with gold braid and pearls. Life size.
Victoria & Albert Museum, London. V&A Images.
© DACS, 2016.

Rachel Whiteread (b. 1963),
Untitled (*Wardrobe*), 1994.

Plaster and glass,
71 x 49¼ x 18¼ in (180 x 125 x 46 cm).
© Rachel Whiteread. Courtesy the artist
and Gagosian Gallery.
(Work destroyed in
MOMART fire 2004.)

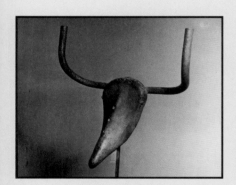

Pablo Picasso (1881–1973),
The Bull, 1942.

Bicycle seat and handles, length 17 in (43 cm)
Photograph by Brassaï (1899–1984), 1943
Musée Picasso, Paris
Sculpture: © Succession Picasso/DACS, London 2016.
Photograph: © Estate Brassaï - RMN-Grand Palais.

Johan Caspar Hendrik Niegeman (1902–1977),
Invitation to the *Bauhaus
Metal Party*, 1929.

Folded card with insert sheet,
10.5 x 14.8 cm (4⅛ x 5⅞ in).
Bauhaus-Archiv Berlin,
Foto: Gunter Lepkowski

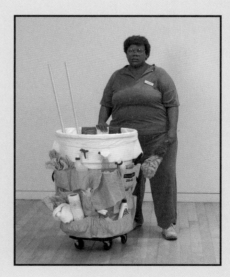

Duane Hanson (1925–1996),
Queenie II, 1988

Autobody filler polychromed in oil, mixed media with
accessories. Variable dimensions.
Gagosian Gallery, © Estate of Duane Hanson/VAGA, New
York/DACS, London 2016.

THANKS!

I would like to thank Laurence King for suggesting that I write something for children. I am extremely grateful to Elizabeth Jenner for her direction and advice, to Donald Dinwiddie for editing the book, and Julia Ruxton for sourcing such great images. A HUGE thanks to Jim Stoten for his incredible illustrations. Many thanks to Angus Hyland for his creative direction and to The Urban Ant for the beautiful design. Finally, I would like to thank Rachel Whiteread for generously giving her time and helping on this book.
—Catherine Ingram 2016

I would like to say thanks to Catherine Ingram, Andrew Rae, Donald Dinwiddie, and Irene Fuga.
—Jim Stoten 2016

CATHERINE INGRAM obtained a First Class Honours degree at Glasgow University. After an MA in 19th Century Art at the Courtauld Institute of Art, Catherine became a graduate scholar at Trinity College, Oxford. On completion of her D.Phil, she was made a Prize Fellow at Magdalen College, Oxford.

JIM STOTEN'S drawings of vast, intricate landscapes filled with tuba-playing elephants, joyful, dancing robots, and crocodiles eating ice cream have featured in commissions for an impressive list of clients including MTV, Habitat, Levi's, Urban Outfitters, and *The Guardian*, while he frequently exhibits his work in galleries around the globe.

LAURENCE KING

Published in 2016 by
Laurence King Publishing
361–373 City Road
London EC1V 1LR
United Kingdom
T +44 20 7841 6900
F +44 20 7841 6910
enquiries@laurenceking.com
www.laurenceking.com

A catalog record for this book is available from the British Library.

ISBN: 978 1 78067 863 4

Printed in China

TO LULU AND SAM, THANKS FOR ALL THE ADVENTURES. WITH LOVE.